V. MALAR
GREATEST HOST OF ALL TIME

V. MALAR
GREATEST HOST OF ALL TIME

Suma Subramaniam

illustrated by
Archana Sreenivasan

CANDLEWICK PRESS

This is a work of fiction. Names, characters, places, and incidents are either products of the author's imagination or, if real, are used fictitiously.

Text copyright © 2024 by Suma Subramaniam
Illustrations copyright © 2024 by Archana Sreenivasan

All rights reserved. No part of this book may be reproduced, transmitted, or stored in an information retrieval system in any form or by any means, graphic, electronic, or mechanical, including photocopying, taping, and recording, without prior written permission from the publisher.

First edition 2024

Library of Congress Catalog Card Number 2024937341
ISBN 978-1-5362-2911-0 (hardcover)
ISBN 978-1-5362-4027-6 (paperback)

24 25 26 27 28 29 SHD 10 9 8 7 6 5 4 3 2 1

Printed in Chelsea, MI, USA

This book was typeset in Filosofia.
The illustrations were created digitally.

Candlewick Press
99 Dover Street
Somerville, Massachusetts 02144

www.candlewick.com

For Amma and Appa, who gave me the gift of a large family
For Srinath, who fills my well with freedom
SS

For Amma, whose sakkarai pongal
is the best I've ever had
AS

CONTENTS

Chapter 1
Ready for Pongal 1

Chapter 2
Guests Arrive 11

Chapter 3
Touring Pori 23

Chapter 4
Preparing for the Festival 35

Chapter 5
It's Time for Bhogi 45

Chapter 6
The Big Celebration 58

Chapter 7
Thai Pongal 67

Chapter 8
Maattu Pongal 79

Chapter 9
Visiting the Local Fair 86

Chapter 10
Kaanum Pongal 99

Glossary 111

Author's Note 118

Chapter One

Ready for Pongal

I TEAR OFF another page from the calendar. Wednesday. It's almost Pongal—finally! I've been dreaming about the harvest festival for weeks.

In Pori, where my parents and I live on our farm, we usually celebrate festivals by singing and dancing to the sounds of the nadaswaram blaring and the thavil beating and booming.

But this year's festival will be different.

All of November, it rained and stormed in our tiny coastal village. In December, the weather got worse: we had a cyclone that formed in the Indian Ocean. Iruttu puyal—the dark storm.

This cyclone season was worse and lasted longer than seasons past. Our rice fields and rivers were destroyed, and some people from our village had to move into the school building for shelter. Luckily, my parents had stocked up on groceries that didn't need to be refrigerated and bought kerosene lanterns so we could see without electricity.

It's mid-January now. The cyclone has finally packed up its trouble and moved out of Pori, and we're slowly recovering. I've been helping my parents by planting and taking care of the animals on our farm, which has been in my family for generations.

Every morning, I feed the cows, birds, and chickens. Even during the storms, I never missed a day of refilling their food and water.

But the most important reason this year's festival will be different is that we'll have guests visiting all the way from the United States! They arrive today, so we've been cleaning the house all day. It's funny because, even though they are family, I've never met these guests before. We've only chatted on the phone and over video. Here's what I know about them:

There's my aunt Selvi: I call her Chithi. She whistles the loudest.

My uncle Muthu: I call him Chithappa. He loves anything and everything to do with computers.

My cousins, Priya and Kamal: Priya is eleven, a year older than me, and Kamal is six. He runs around making faces and never sits still. Priya does most of the talking during our video chats.

"The last time your uncle visited India, you had just turned one," Amma told me last night. "And this is Priya and Kamal's first visit."

I rolled my fingertip across the Arabian Sea and the Pacific Ocean on my grandfather's antique globe.

"This is where they live." I showed Amma the bindi I had stuck on Seattle. "So far away." I sighed and bit my fingernails.

"What's troubling you, kanna?" Amma asked.

I didn't answer. I don't talk much when I'm anxious, but she could guess what I was feeling. As much as I have been curious about my cousins, I had to wonder how we would get along in real life. I wasn't sure if they would want to be friends with me—or vice versa.

"Atithi devo bhava, Malar Velayudham," Amma said, using my full name. Usually, everyone calls me Malar, or V. Malar. "Remember, we will treat our guests like gods, no matter what." Amma shook her index finger at me like I was about to do something wrong. "While they are here, I want you to behave like your name, Malar."

Malar means "flower." My parents named me that because they're both agriculturists, so they know a lot about planting, growing, and farming, of course. Velayudham is my father's name.

I love my name—it's just right for me because I love flowers, especially the lotus. The lotus has a special gift, you see. Appa says its roots are anchored strong and deep in the ground. Every night, it closes its petals and submerges into the dark river water. In the morning, it rises and bursts into blooms under the sunlight.

"I'll be nice to Priya and Kamal," I said to Amma last night. "Promise."

"Your chithappa is all the family your father has, kanna, and he hasn't seen him in years. You must think beyond yourself while they're here. Understood?"

I stared down at the globe and nodded. Appa was thirteen and Chithappa was only five when their parents passed away. "I'll try," I said.

As I'm retying the bow in my hair, Amma calls me to the kitchen. "Hurry, Malar! Our guests will be here this afternoon. One. Two. Three. Joot!"

Amma sweeps the kitchen. Appa scrubs the floor. I brush, wipe, and dust until Amma agrees that everything is sparkling clean.

When the bells from the temple down the street ring, we gather around the table, which once belonged to my grandmother, for a mid-morning snack. Amma sets out clay soup bowls. The paruthi paal sizzles warm in the pot. Amma ground the soaked cottonseeds this morning to get their milk, then cooked it with jaggery and ginger. Cottonseed milk is one of my favorite drinks.

"Chellam, we're going to have a super-o-super Pongal with our special guests, aren't we?" Appa asks me.

I nod. I love it when Appa calls me his dear one. I am looking forward to laughing and playing with my cousins, but it feels complicated. "What if they don't like it here? What if they're annoying and use all my things and make a mess?"

Amma adds another ladle of milk to my bowl. "Pongal is about spreading love and cheer. And it will be good to learn to share with your cousins."

"Priya and Kamal live in a big house. They must have everything. They don't need to play with my things."

"When we share, our hearts expand and the joy of the festival doubles," Appa says. "They're

family, chellam. Do you know how to show your love for them?"

Before I can answer, Amma responds, "By letting them eat first."

"By helping them when they don't understand how things work here," Appa says.

I swallow the paal in my mouth. "By offering them my things."

Amma smiles. "But the most important of all, Malar, is to treat them the way you want to be treated, kanna," she says, calling me the pupil of her eye.

"I hope Priya and Kamal like me and our village."

"They will," Amma insists. "You just have to be patient with them."

I don't know if I have it in me to be patient, but Pongal is meant to renew life and give us hope. So I make a decision. I'm going to be sure our guests have a great visit while we celebrate the festival together.

"I'll be the best host, a super-host!" I say.

I drink up the rest of the cottonseed milk. But deep inside, I know that patience is like the fragile clay soup bowl I hold in my hand—easy to break and hard to repair.

Chapter Two

Guests Arrive

HONK! HONK!

At noon, we hear a loud horn outside the window.

"Did you hear that, chellam?" Appa shouts. "They have arrived."

A bus pulls up at the stop a few hundred feet from our house. I run out the door, through the garden, and pull open the metal gate.

I put on my best smile and stand on my tiptoes as people step off the bus.

"Malar!" Priya cries, jumping out of the vehicle. "We're here!"

Amma said guests are like gods, so I join my palms in welcome. "Vanakkam! Vaanga! Vaanga!"

Priya is full of energy and speaks like an express train. I don't understand her completely, but I catch "meet finally" and something about this trip being a goat.

"Goat?" I look around. "I don't see a goat."

She laughs. "It means Greatest of All Time!"

I think that means she's happy to meet me, but she's talking too fast, mixing Tamil and English with a strange accent. I've heard her speak like this on video chat, but it's even more difficult to understand now due to her excitement.

Behind Priya is Kamal. Then Chithi and Chithappa get off the bus.

"We've missed you all," Chithi says.

I run to hug her.

"Instead of hiring a car, we thought the kids should experience the train and bus for the first time," Chithappa says. "Hey, podisu! Come here, little one!" He picks me up and does a twirl.

"Haiya!" I tell him.

"Finally you're here." Amma hugs Chithi.

Appa embraces his brother. "We have plenty to catch up on, Thambi!"

I take a closer look at my cousins. Priya wears a T-shirt and really short shorts. Kamal wears jeans.

Priya is looking at me, too. I'm wearing a long skirt and a blouse. She crosses her arms and holds her chin up high. "I'm the tallest."

I look at Kamal's curly head and Priya's ponytail. "My hair is the longest," I say, swinging my braid.

"Whatever." Priya shrugs. "I'm the oldest."

She's right about that at least, so I smile and grab her hand. "Come on. I have so much to show you two."

Back at the house, Amma puts out a big plate of murukku for everyone in the living room.

Priya grabs a fried snack from the tray. "Ooh! I want the crunchies."

Kamal pounces on the tray next. Amma says I should always use my manners, especially when we have guests, so I wait until everyone has claimed a snack and then take only one.

Amma's murukku are the best. I devour the handmade fried lentil cracker in a minute. It's hard not to go for another. But she made them special for Priya, Kamal, Chithi, and Chithappa.

Appa makes fresh coffee for all the adults while I make Priya and Kamal my favorite drink. "This is badam paal, spiced almond milk," I say.

Priya looks into the cup and shakes her head.

"I want juice," Kamal says.

I try not to be too disappointed that Priya and Kamal don't taste the drink I made for them.

But Chithi is attentive to everything. She doesn't wear a sari like Amma. Her dupatta is pinned neatly to her chudidhar. And when Amma gives her a string of jasmine to clip to her hair, she bows her head in gratitude.

Chithi cups the flowers in her palm and holds them up to her nose. "Madurai malli . . . mmm. Do you want some, Priya?"

Priya dismisses her mother and points her finger at me. "You said you'd show me around."

Priya and Kamal follow me to my bedroom with their bags.

"Not bad," Priya says when she sees my art on the wall. "Nice colors on the temple."

She thinks my art is not bad. *I* think my art is great! I wonder how good an artist Priya is.

Priya unpacks her luggage, pulling out her clothes. Jeans. T-shirts. Shorts. She has so many pairs of jeans! I've never worn jeans in my life. In fact, none of the girls in my village wear jeans because they can be expensive, and skirts and blouses are considered traditional.

Priya eyes the holes in the hem of my skirt. The skirt was given to me by an older girl on my street.

When I grow out of my dresses, I pass them down to younger girls. Amma says it's a good way to use less stuff, respect the environment, and learn how to give and receive. Priya's ripped jeans make me wonder if they are hand-me-downs, too, but I don't ask her.

She grabs her pile of clothes and dumps them on my desk.

"Haiyo! Don't leave your things everywhere."

But Priya doesn't listen. She reaches into the pile and fishes out a package wrapped in blue and green paper. "Hey," she says to Kamal. "Want to give this to Malar?"

"A gift for me?" I ask.

Priya and Kamal smile.

I untie the ribbon and open the gift. Tucked under soft tissue paper is delicious goodness.

I fling myself at her. Priya hugs me back.

"Chocolates. My favorite! Thank you."

"Um . . . truffles," Priya says.

I share the truffles with them and gobble one up. "Yummy."

When I show them all my favorite things around my room, Priya says that her room is bigger than mine. She even brags that her bookshelf is bigger than mine. And Kamal adds that his globe is bigger than mine.

And just like that, I realize how annoying Priya and Kamal can be.

I decide to take them outside and introduce them to our animals. First, I bring them over to Raja and Rani's coop.

"Hey, roosty! Hey, chicky!" Priya calls out to them.

Raja squawks. Rani screams. They don't trust the new guests.

"He's Raja. And she's Rani," I correct her. "See how their beaks are like a parrot's? Curved like a hook. That's why they're called kili-mooku seval. They take a while to be friends. They have to believe that you won't hurt them."

"Raja, the roosty! Rani, the chicky!" Priya yells.

"Raja, the roosty! Rani, the chicky!" Kamal repeats after her.

The chickens flap their wings, so I turn toward the cowshed.

"Lakshmi! Gowri!" I call to the cow and calf. "Look, we have guests."

Gowri is lying on the ground, chewing grass. Lakshmi is standing near the fence. The animals turn around and acknowledge me, but they don't come over to meet my cousins.

"Lakshmi is a strong Bargur. That's where she gets her brown skin with white markings. You should taste her milk. It's thick and delicious. Her calf Gowri just turned one a few weeks ago. You should see them trot together."

"Cows that trot? Like ponies?" Priya laughs.

I make a face but squash down my irritation. Kamal tries to squeeze through the fence into their pen. "Careful," I say, pulling him back. "You can pet them tomorrow when they are more comfortable with your voices."

Priya whispers something into Kamal's ear.

"Ewwww!" Kamal screws up his face.

"I know." Priya nods. "Gross!"

"What is it?" I ask.

Priya shakes her head and doesn't say anything.

We go back to the house and into my bedroom.

"Tiny house," Priya says.

"Tiny room," Kamal says.

"Tiny everything," Priya says.

I can feel the angry heat on my face, but I don't want to shout at them. I'm on a mission—a mission to be a super-host.

"Not everything is tiny here." I put my hands on my hips. "We have a big yard. Big chickens. An even bigger cow. Big farm. Big fields. Big trees.

Big river. Big temples. So many big things. I'll show you."

But Priya's response is all about Seattle. Seattle this. Seattle that. I tune out what Priya is saying because now it's starting to feel like my house, my farm, and I are nothing at all compared to Seattle.

Amma and Chithi enter the room. "What a refreshing change," Chithi says, "to see the rainbow of colored houses on the street here, and not a dull gray Seattle sky." She smiles at me, and I feel her warmth.

She looks at Priya. "Do you have something to say to your cousin?" she prompts.

Priya gives me a snide glance and twirls her ponytail. "Thanks for sharing your room with us."

I think about my promise to be a super-host. "You're welcome," I say, smiling so hard my face hurts.

Chapter Three

Touring Pori

LATER THAT AFTERNOON, Amma and Chithi take us out on a stroll to our local temple of the goddess Mariamman.

On the walk there, Priya and Kamal are quiet except when they're filling each other's ears with secrets, and then they let out loud giggles.

Their laughter makes my whole body cringe. But I notice Priya's eyes widen and she stops laughing and whispering when she sees the temple's stone pillars and sculptures.

"South Indian marvels," Chithi tells Priya. "Look at these intricate engravings. They've weathered many generations and storms, including the recent cyclone."

"What's a cyclone?" Kamal asks.

"It's a hurricane," Priya says.

"A tropical hurricane." I explain what I learned in school. "Hurricanes are storms that form over the Atlantic and Northeast Pacific. Cyclones form over the South Pacific and Indian Ocean."

Amma nods. "Smart answer," she says as we walk toward the Nagaraja shrine.

"Look at this fig tree—so big and ancient!" Chithi points out. "And different from the redwood and fir trees in the Pacific Northwest."

I immediately look at Priya. But she doesn't react to what Chithi said. "Careful," I warn them. "You might see a naga."

"Eww! A snake?" Priya scrunches up her face in fear.

"Most temples have an anthill or a termite mound where the serpent god lives. I've only seen him once, but if we ignore him, he won't do anything to us. The snake isn't poisonous."

Priya smirks at me. "You mean venomous. Something is only poisonous when you eat it. Venomous means the snake could poison you with his bite."

I try hard not to roll my eyes, but Priya has already moved on. "This temple looks so old," she says.

"Romba pazhasu," I say.

"In English," Priya reminds me. "Everyone speaks so fast in Tamil here. I can hardly understand it."

"It's ancient. At least five hundred years old. It was built by a king," I tell them.

Kamal doesn't pay much attention to the temple as we walk around. He's too busy watching out for the snake.

But when we finish the tour, he declares, "I'm done with temples."

"Me too," says Priya.

And I'm done hanging out with my cousins, I think, even though there's so much more of Pori to show them.

The Kaveri River and the boats.

The fields and crops.

The family with a new baby girl on our street who said, "Bring your cousins over to see the baby."

The old couple next door to us who said, "We can tell them stories about Pori."

Then Priya says, "Four more days before we return to civilization."

I smile and play the role of super-host and say, "Four days before you'll leave with lots of great memories."

"Chithi and I are going back to the fields," Amma announces. "Stay as long as you want and then join us."

"Let's go play," I urge as Amma and Chithi walk away.

But Priya and Kamal refuse to come with me.

"My legs ache. I wanna go with Amma," Kamal whines. "I'm tired."

"Me too," Priya says. "I wanna nap so bad."

"I wanna play video games," Kamal says.

"No video games or napping!" I snap.

"Hey, I'm the oldest here, okay?" Priya says. "I'll decide what we do."

I should hold my tongue. But I don't.

"You think you're the boss in my village?" I say, my voice getting louder. "Well, you're wrong. Podi!"

"Did you tell me to go away? You're mean," Priya says.

"You are too," I say.

We stare at each other.

In my head, I count backward from ten to one to calm myself down.

Priya acts like nothing here is good enough, not my village, my home, or my anything.

But, I remember, here in Pori, we treat our guests like gods, and I'm supposed to be a super-host.

"Okay. I'm sorry," I tell Priya. "Let's go. Nap and video games after we stop at the fields."

"Ha!" Priya smirks. "I win."

I grit my teeth and clench my fists as we walk along the slick Kaveri riverbank toward the paddy fields. Priya and Kamal clutch each other so they don't fall.

Sunset paints the sky a rose-milk pink when we reach the field. A cool breeze sweeps over the crops and treetops, making them sway. Crows caw and sparrows chirp along the groves of coconut palms, banana plants, sugarcane, and tamarind trees. The buzzing of dragonflies and mosquitoes rises up around us. Priya, Kamal, and I run between the rows of tall, heavy sugarcane plants. The dry grass pokes our feet. Even though the farm can be a lot of work, I love the plants and crops we have.

I show Priya and Kamal our compost pile.

"This is what makes our soil rich with nutrients," I tell them.

I dig my hands in and hold out a clump of the compost.

"So many worms." Priya squirms, staring down at the earthworms crawling across my palms. She pushes me away.

I drop the worms back into the pile and wash my hands at the nearby well.

Then Amma comes over with a sugarcane and hands each of us a piece to chew.

Priya holds the peeled sugarcane to her nose. "How do you eat this thing?"

"Chew it and spit out the fiber," I say.

"Here you go." Chithi hands us a banana leaf for the waste.

"Sweet." Kamal's mischievous eyes ignite as he chews.

"These last couple months were supposed to be our planting season for beets, gourds, ladies' finger, turnips, pumpkins, and chilies," she says.

Priya laughs. "Ladies' finger?"

"Okra, sweetie," Chithi tells her. "Vendakkai. We call it ladies' finger in India."

"I hate okra," Priya says. "It's slimy."

"I love it," I say. "It's my favorite vegetable."

I wish I could stuff a bowl of vegetable curry into Priya's mouth. Then she would have to stop talking and admit how tasty okra can be.

Amma continues talking. "But we couldn't get anything planted during the cyclone."

"Thanks to Mariamman, the goddess of our village"—Chithi joins her palms and looks up at the evening sky—"the cyclone is behind us now."

"We may not have much of a vegetable yield this season," Amma adds, "but we can still make the most of what we have. Especially for Pongal, when we celebrate nature."

"And nature celebrates us," Chithi reminds us, and winks at me. "Priya and Kamal know very little about Pongal. You'll have to teach them everything."

Although the morning started off with high hopes, by now I feel like I've lost my voice and my smile. But as we talk about the spirit of the festival, I start to feel my heart lift. Pongal is also about celebrating our bloodline. I look at Priya's and Kamal's faces, and I see how similar we look. All of us with our thick, curly hair, sharing the same skin color, the same pointed noses and high cheekbones like our grandmother's. Priya and Kamal are indeed my family, and being nice to family is not a chore.

"Let's go home now, kids," Amma says.

"Finally." Priya jumps up and down.

Amma holds my hand. Her warmth is the balm I need. I hold Chithi's hand. Chithi holds Priya's hand, and Priya holds Kamal's.

Tomorrow will be a better day for us all.

I hope.

Chapter Four

Preparing for the Festival

WHEN I WAKE up, Priya and Kamal are fast asleep on the mat. The morning is peaceful like the Kaveri River, like my home usually is.

I tiptoe out to the front room. Nobody's there. Amma and Chithi are busy in the kitchen, arguing about how many chilies to add to the sambar.

"Five," Amma says.

"Haiyo. Just two, please, Akka." Chithi chuckles. "My kids are not used to so much spice."

Amma and Chithi agree to set aside a portion of the lentil soup for Priya and Kamal and add the chilies to the rest of it.

Appa and Chithappa are out in the front porch, discussing politics.

"Vaa inga. Come here, podisu," Chithappa says when he sees me. "You're up early like the rising sun."

I can understand him and Chithi much more easily than I do Priya and Kamal. My aunt and uncle's accent is like mine. I smile when he offers me his hand. When Chithappa shakes my hand, he's telling me he loves me.

Chithappa is like my own father in many ways. He doesn't talk much, but he smiles often, and he doesn't call me by my name. Instead, he calls me "little one."

Chithappa tells me I should come visit them in the summer.

"We can go to Mount Rainier together. It's not as high as Everest, but it's beautiful," he says. He shows me pictures from his phone, and I wish I could transport myself to Rainier instantly.

"Someday we'll visit Seattle," Appa says, and I wonder what that would be like as I walk around to the side of the house.

I grab a handful of millet, climb up the ladder, and check the terra-cotta sparrow nest hanging outside my bedroom window. Inside the clump of hay and feathers are four little eggs. I drop the millet into the nest for the sparrow family to eat.

As I climb down the ladder, I hear footsteps and a voice.

"Hey, Malar, what are you doing?" Priya talks through her yawns, and I can feel it: the peace of the morning is about to be disturbed. Kamal stands behind her.

I point to the nest. "I just put some food in the nest for the sparrows up there. Come on. Let's go pick some leaves."

To my surprise, Priya beams. "Cool! I like to climb trees."

Kamal stretches his arms. His face looks fresh, and he seems to have had a good night's sleep.

"What kind of leaves?" Priya asks.

"Neem, mango, banana, and maruthaani leaves," I say.

"To feed the cows?" she asks.

"Neem leaves ward off spiders," I tell them both. "Mango leaves to make a bunting for the front door. Banana leaves to serve lunch on. And maruthaani for our hands."

"So many uses for leaves," Priya says. "Interesting."

I'm not sure what she means by "interesting."

"The one for the hands . . ." Priya pauses. "Do you mean henna?"

"Henna's what they call it in North India."

She shakes her head. "I call it henna, too."

"Here, it's maruthaani," I say.

"Henna," she says.

"Maruthaani," I say again.

"Henna! Henna! Henna!" she chants.

I bury my face into my palms as if it will take away my cousin's taunts.

"Fine. Let's go." I lead them to the backyard.

Priya and I climb up the mango tree and begin picking. Kamal gathers the leaves on the ground.

Then we move to the other plants, chatting as we pick.

Afterward, we make bouquets of neem leaves and place them over the shelves in all the rooms.

"This wards off evil energies from the house. Evil, evil, go away!" I shout.

Kamal laughs.

"That's silly," Priya says.

It's hard not to feel like it's them against me, even though we were just getting along so well. I try to remember I'm a super-host.

"Do you know how to make a string of leaves?" I ask Priya.

She shakes her head.

"I'll show you." I set the cluster of mango leaves on the floor.

I pull out some broomstick fronds and give them each a pair of scissors. We sit down next to the leaves.

I wrap a mango leaf over a long jute string. Then I poke one of the tiny pieces of the frond through the leaf until it holds on to the string. I repeat the process. Priya and Kamal follow my instructions and help me finish the rest of the leaf decoration.

"Leaves are cool," Kamal says.

I lean over to him. "And so are you."

He doesn't reply, but he smiles shyly at me.

"You hang up one side, and I'll do the other," I say to Priya when we finish.

She climbs up the ladder. I give her one end of the string to pin to the right side of the front door. When she's done, I pull the ladder to the left side and pin up the other end of the bunting. "Our entrance is ready."

We stand together and look up at our decoration.

"We're a good team," Priya says.

Team. The peaceful word passes through my ears and settles in my heart like the morning quiet. It makes me feel like I have won today.

In the afternoon, my cousins play on their tablets.

"I'm going to help Amma with the maruthaani," I say to Priya.

She keeps her eyes glued to her screen. "You're missing out on a cool video game."

I calm the shouting voice inside me and say, "Haiyo, Priya, you're going to miss out on something even more cool."

I sit on the kitchen floor with Amma. I drop the maruthaani leaves onto the grinding stone. Amma adds the juice of a lemon, a couple of drops of turpentine oil, and a teaspoon of sugar to the leaves. I grind everything to a paste.

Then I pull out a roll of cellophane paper. Amma runs scissors along the sheet and cuts it into squares. We roll the squares and curl them in a loop to form cones. We fill the cones with henna.

Then Amma draws peacocks on my palms.

Priya walks in. "Ooh. I want some, too," she says.

"Me three," says Kamal, following.

They dump their tablets and sit beside me. Amma draws flowers on Priya's palms and the sun on Kamal's. Then we don't touch anything while our hands dry.

"My back itches," Kamal says.

"My neck itches," adds Priya.

"My nose itches," I say. "You scratch my nose with the tip of your finger, and I'll scratch your neck with mine."

Priya scrunches up her face. "I'll scratch Kamal, and he'll scratch me."

"What happened to our team spirit from the morning?" I nudge her.

But Priya doesn't respond.

We're not friends yet, I guess, but maybe we still can be? The festival has only just begun, so maybe if I try hard enough, I can still be the best Pongal super-host of Pori.

Chapter Five
It's Time for Bhogi

"THE SUN is about to go down over the river." Appa begins to clear a space in the front yard. "Time for Bhogi."

"So it's not Pongal?" Priya shakes her head, confused.

"Pongal is four days. Today is Bhogi," I say.

"Bhogi. Sounds like *yogi*." Priya laughs and Kamal giggles.

I'm annoyed, but I stay calm in front of Appa. "Bhogi is the first day. Today we put away old, torn,

and broken things, and dance around a fire . . ."
I pause for a moment. "*Fire* sounds like *wire.*"

"You liar." Priya laughs.

I put my hands on my hips. "Who's a liar?"

"Just kidding. Easy, girl." Priya glances my way and winks. "Worked with the rhyme. This celebration is kinda long."

"It'll be over before we know it, chellam," Appa says. "And now we're going to make a big bonfire."

"For real?" Priya asks.

Appa smiles and tugs at his beard. "Let's do it together. Here's what we'll need—twigs, sticks, bark, logs, and manure."

"What do you mean, manure?" Priya asks.

"Cow dung," I say to her.

Kamal squirms. "Poop? Yuck!"

"Manure is full of nutrients for the farm, and it's the best source of fuel for fire, kanna," Appa says.

Priya and Kamal follow me to the backyard, where Amma and Chithi are making fresh dung cakes. Amma mixes the manure with water and a little bit of hay, charcoal, and ash to make a thick paste in large buckets in the yard.

Chithi shapes handfuls of paste into patties.

"Eww! Mommy, I can't believe you're touching poop," Priya squeals.

"It's not so bad, sweetie. And I'm not actually touching the poop. See?" Chithi lifts up her gloved hands.

"These will take a week to dry," Amma says as she sets the dung cakes out on a large sheet under the sun. "But there are plenty of dried ones in the bucket over there." She points to a container in the corner of the yard.

"I'm not touching those things." Priya plugs her nose.

Kamal does the same and speaks quickly in English.

"What's he saying?" I ask Priya.

"'Gross.' It means disgusting in case you're wondering."

I shrug. "You poop. I poop. We all poop. Cows are great poopers. Ours poop ten to fifteen times a day."

"Enough of the poop talk, weirdo." Priya shakes her head.

"Okay. I'll carry the manure. You two can collect the coconut fronds, bark, and sticks," I say.

I pull out the wheelbarrow from the shed. Priya watches me so closely, I feel like I'm always about to say or do something wrong or mean or both.

"I'll push the wheelbarrow," Priya says.

"Are you sure?" I ask.

"One hundred."

But in a couple of minutes, she's struggling to balance it with the extra weight of the manure.

"You can do it," I cheer.

Priya uses all her strength to push, but the wheelbarrow is so heavy it tips over against one of the buckets of dung water.

The bucket topples and the water spills all over her.

"Yuck! Gross!" she cries.

Kamal bursts out laughing.

"Shhh, Kamal!" Chithi tries to hush him. He doesn't stop.

Priya's face is red. I try my best not to laugh when she stares at me with smoldering magma eyes.

I extend my arms to help Priya up, but she pushes me away. She grits her teeth, clenches her fists, and starts screaming and crying. She reminds me of the cyclone.

I stop staring and pick up the sun-dried dung pies one by one while Priya cries. I wheel them out to the open space in the yard, where Appa and Chithappa made a circle with bricks and stones for the bonfire.

When I'm done, I look at Priya, who's finally stopped crying. "Do you want to clean up?" I ask her.

She refuses to answer me.

"It's not a big deal. Look!" I pick up a cup of dung water and pour it over my head.

Everyone stares at me, then bursts out laughing.

"See?" I tell Priya. "It's fun!"

And Priya finally giggles.

She gets to her feet. We wash off in the water from the tap while Amma and Chithi bring us fresh sets of clothes. We change and get back to helping Appa make fire.

We add bark, sticks, coconut fronds, logs, and the manure to the pyre. Then Appa breaks off pieces of dried wood and creates a spindle and a hearth board out of them.

"We must make sure the spindle is straight and as thick as my thumb," he says, and measures its length. "Eight inches. Good."

"Now we wait," Chithappa says.

The entire family gathers in a circle around the pyre.

Appa hands the spindle and hearth board to me. He tells me to apply pressure on the spindle. I scrape and drill it into the hearth board over a clump of dried coconut frond. I drill, and drill, and drill until the coal forms and grows, and we see smoke.

"How long is this going to take?" Kamal asks.

"Shhhh!" Appa hushes. "Patience. We need to hear it."

No one makes a sound. Not even a cough or a laugh. I keep drilling. Appa pats down the clump of coconut frond enough so it doesn't get caught in the spindle.

Scrape and drill. Back and forth. Back and forth.

Breathe.

Scrape and drill. Back and forth. Back and forth.

Then...

CRACK!

A warm spark crackles.

"You made fire!" yells Kamal.

"Whoa, you're the GOAT!" Priya says in a low, soft voice.

"Super-o-super! Bring all the old things you can find," Appa announces.

We pull out everything that's worn-out or dry. Amma and Chithi bring cracked mud pots. Chithappa brings a broken branch. Kamal adds twigs. Priya helps me carry dried hay and leaves.

We throw all the things into the bonfire one by one.

Appa joins his palms. "We honor Indra—the king of the gods—and pray to Varuna—the god of rains. Let's thank them for a year of rice and grains."

We bow to the clouds.

"We must replace bad habits with good ones. Let's each make a promise," Amma tells us.

"Kandippa!" Chithi agrees. "Remember the saying . . . one good deed is worth a thousand intentions?"

Priya promises to be more patient with Kamal.

Kamal promises to eat one candy a day instead of four.

I promise to be less angry when things don't work out my way.

"Let's all make a promise together as a family," Appa urges.

"To share," Amma says.

"To care and be more kind," Chithi says.

"To laugh often," Chithappa says.

"And to love," Amma says, smiling over at me.

Then Appa brings out the tape recorder.

"What's that?" Priya asks.

"It plays music," I say.

"You mean like a tablet or something?" Priya asks.

"Aamaa. Yeah! Wait until you hear it." I press play.

Drums beat. A voice booms from the speakers, and a Tamil film song fills the air.

"Thalaiva," Appa shouts, using the nickname for the movie actor Rajinikanth.

Chithi whistles. We all join hands and circle the bonfire. A mild drizzle mists the evening as neighbors and friends join our celebration. Everybody claps, dances, and sings around the fire.

Priya's hands and feet fly up and down as the music stirs, strikes, and sparks with the beat. At one point, she wraps her arms around mine and hugs me. We look at each other for a second. She smiles. I hug her back.

"You're a good dancer," I say. "You've got to teach me your moves."

"Don't go being all nice to me now." She laughs. "But sure, why not?"

I mimic her swinging moves. Even Kamal flaps his arms in the air and jumps.

The bad feelings I had for them burn down like the ashes in the bonfire. The discomfort between us is fading. In its place, I think a new kind of friendship is being born.

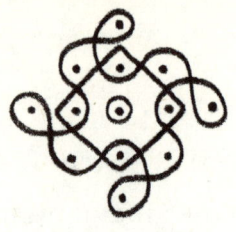

Chapter Six

The Big Celebration

I WAKE UP STICKY from sweat, but the heat doesn't bother me as much as the snoring and other sounds that come with sharing my bedroom with Priya and Kamal.

I glance at the clock. It's only five.

The house is still dark, and the sun hasn't risen yet. Everyone is asleep except Amma and Appa. "Today's a good day for Thai Pongal," I hear Appa telling Amma as I enter the kitchen.

Appa lights the kerosene lamps while Amma washes the dishes in the sink.

Then she begins to cook, wasting no time. She has already chosen the freshest vegetables and assembled them all on the counter. We don't have the usual winter melons this year because of the cyclone, so she has replaced them with pumpkin. She has replaced carrots with pulses and fresh peas with dried ones. Humming a Sanskrit hymn, she pulls out the raw spices from the cabinets and sets them on the grinding stone.

Today is Thai Pongal. It's also called Uzhavar Thirunal and is my favorite day of the harvest festival. All the work the farmers do throughout the year leads up to this day.

"Growing our own food is important, chellam," Appa always says. "Even in our darkest times, we can depend on ourselves. We can live on what we produce."

I head over to the altar. On the shelf lies my new dress, covered with newspaper to keep it clean. I can see the peacock green on the edge, the zari border, and the lovely folds on the skirt.

I get a new dress three times a year—for my birthday, in July; for Pongal; and for Deepavali, the festival of lights. That's a lot compared to my parents. They buy clothes for themselves only for Deepavali. I can tell it's different for Priya and Kamal, because they seem to own a lot of clothing.

"Malar?" Amma's voice is sweet-sounding this morning. "V. Malar, there's so much work to do. Go get a shower, then come help out," she says.

I shower, dress, and get ready. By then my aunt and uncle are awake, too. The street outside is already alive and buzzing with people walking around, carrying out their morning chores. The sky doesn't have even a wisp of gray in the clouds. Everyone's wearing colorful clothes: the men in shirts and veshtis, the women in saris.

When Priya wakes up, she sits on the mat and complains about how her skin is sticky with sweat.

She whines that the heat makes her tired and thirsty.

She tells me that she'd take the rain in Seattle over this heat any day.

"You should stop complaining about India and enjoy the warmth on your skin," I say.

I want to tell her that Pongal is about gratitude.

Pongal is celebrating what we have.

Pongal is doing things together.

Pongal is replacing bad habits with good ones.

Pongal is about abundance.

Pongal marks the beginning of something beautiful.

But I don't think she'll want to hear any of that.

Priya sighs. "You don't get it."

"Get what?"

"That I miss home," she says in a low voice.

Guilt churns my stomach and flows upward through my chest. It settles in my throat. I want to tell her that sometimes her words feel like thorns to me, that I can't seem to break down the wall between us. But instead, I bite the inside of my lip.

Priya can barely contain her frustration over my silence. "Someday, Malar, someday," she mumbles, "I hope you come to Seattle and then you'll see what I'm talking about."

"Someday, Priya, I will." I pat-pat her hand. "I can't wait to get to know more about Seattle. But today, we can't be sad. It's Thai Pongal."

Priya makes a face like she disagrees and shrugs. I clear my throat and turn to Kamal, who is still lying on the mat with a sheet over him.

"Sleepyhead," I tease Kamal.

I try to wake him up, but he doesn't budge. I lift his eyelids. He closes them tight.

"You know why Kamal doesn't want to wake up?" Priya whispers. "It's nighttime in Seattle. He has jet lag."

My eyes widen. "Jet lag?"

Priya nods. "It affects people's sleep when they travel across time zones."

"Is that why you both were so sleepy yesterday and the day before?"

"Yes, and that's why we stayed in a hotel in Chennai for a few days before traveling here," Priya says.

I get it now. Everything this morning is happening when it's night in Seattle.

I look at Kamal again. I put the sheet back over his face and let him sleep. "Okay, you don't have to get up."

"By the way, your skirt is so pretty." Priya checks me out from top to bottom. "I left all my Indian clothes in Seattle. I only wear them for Indian gatherings or Indian shows. But now I wish I had them here."

It was fun when Priya showed me her dance steps last evening. How her waist bent like the coconut trees during the attack of the cyclone. Now that I know how lovely she can be when she's in her element, the upside-down curve of her lips makes me sad, too.

I open my drawer and pull out a skirt and blouse. I give them to her. "Here, you can wear mine."

A spark brightens Priya's eyes. She smiles.

"Ooh! Are you sure?" she asks.

I want to ask her, Will you share your jeans with me? And will you stop whispering secrets into Kamal's ear? And will you stop bossing me around?

But I hold myself back. Instead, I nod and smile. Priya beams. The skirt is chili red, with swans. Priya looks gorgeous in it. Though she's older than me, we're almost the same size.

"You can keep them," I tell her. "Take them to Seattle with you."

Priya gasps. "For real?" She hugs me tight. "You really are the GOAT!"

We go to the living room, where Amma ties strings of jasmine around our braids and hooks silver anklets on our feet. Chithi draws bindis on our foreheads and slips colorful matching bangles onto our wrists. We hold each other's hands and stare at the mirror. We look alike now.

Finally, Kamal gets out of bed. Our bangles and anklets jingle-jangle as we chase him around the house until he showers and gets ready.

"Hurry up, girls," Amma says. "Go draw a kolam. We'll begin our celebrations soon."

"A kolam?" Priya asks.

"Come with me." I grip her hand. "We can make one together!"

Chapter Seven

Thai Pongal

PRIYA AND I step off the front porch carrying steel bowls brimming with rice powder.

The whole street is adorned with beautiful, large kolams.

I was six when I learned to draw my first kolam. After that, Amma insisted that I should practice by drawing a small kolam every day. So I would practice a small pattern on the ground—sometimes a bird, sometimes a flower.

"Don't you ever draw a kolam outside your house in Seattle?" I ask Priya.

"Never." Priya shakes her head. "Amma has these shiny thingies she puts out on special days. They're pretty, but they're not like these." She gestures to the explosions of colors and patterns on the street.

I know what to draw at the threshold of our house this morning—a large lotus. Priya watches me carefully as I dot the ground with the rice powder and connect the dots until the flower forms.

"Wow, you're fast," she remarks. "It already looks good. What's it going to be?"

I make a thick, deep brick-red paste from mixing the colored rice powder with a few drops of water. "It's a lotus. Like the meaning of Kamal's name. It's my favorite flower." I show her how to border the lotus design with the paste. "Want to try?"

It takes us an hour to complete our kolam. My legs hurt. My back hurts. But when Priya leans over and says, "Our kolam is amazing!" it feels like it was all worth it.

We pick up the empty bowls and stand there, marveling at our creation.

Suddenly, we hear a noise. It's not Raja, the rooster, or Rani, the hen, squawking. It's not Lakshmi and Gowri mooing. It's not anybody shouting on the street. It's not a bus. It's not a rickshaw.

It's a scream coming from inside the house.

"Akkaaaaaaaaaaaaaaaaa!"

It's Kamal calling for Priya. I turn around and my stomach twists.

Kamal runs toward us like a thunderstorm gaining ground. There's no time to react. Kamal kicks open the gate and crashes into us.

"Siva! Siva!" I shout, as if the god who is meant to destroy the universe will save us.

We all fall.

"Haiyo!"

"Owwie!"

"Ouch!"

The next moment, all that remains of the beautiful kolam is a big circle of mud, colored powder, and dirt on the ground. Our heads, faces, and clothes are covered in kolam powder and dirt.

I can't speak. My eyes burn and I feel Priya and Kamal's weight on me.

Kamal laughs like a lion cub. He doesn't get it.

Anger rushes through my stomach all the way to my lips like a balloon that is about to burst. I'm so mad at Kamal.

I hold him by his shoulders. "This is not funny, Kamal. The kolam we made was a lotus—just like your name."

"He's just a kid, Malar. Remember the promises we all made last evening during Bhogi?" Priya says. "I promised to be more patient with Kamal."

I can barely control my anger, but I grind my teeth and don't let it get the best of me. I hear a voice echoing to me from deep inside.

Forgive.

"And I promised to be less angry when things don't work out my way. The kolam didn't work out. It's okay. We have so much more to do today," I say.

I don't look back at the mess. We dust our clothes off and wash our hands and faces.

Inside, Chithi stands behind Amma and winks at me, but Amma is really upset when she sees us.

"What did you do to yourselves?" Amma asks. "I thought you went out to draw a kolam."

I nestle into the crook of her arm.

"It was—" I begin, but Priya cuts me off.

"An accident." She raises her voice. "We tripped over each other."

Kamal looks down at the floor. He doesn't say anything.

"Yeah, but—" I begin again.

"You need to be more careful, Malar. Go get cleaned up. All of you," Amma says.

I open my mouth to explain, but Priya hushes me.

I don't say another word. My jaw tightens. I run into my bedroom and grab my drawing book and colored pencils. Carrying them with me, I dash out into the backyard and settle down on a pile of hay with Lakshmi and Gowri nearby.

Priya and Kamal follow me into the yard, but Priya's too scared of the animals to enter the cowshed. I put my head down and focus on the paper in front of me. Tears prick at my eyes.

Priya places her arm on the wooden railing and leans in as far as she can. "Of course, it was Kamal's fault. But he's my little brother. I had to defend him."

"I need space," I say to her.

"I know you're sad about the kolam. I am, too," Priya says.

I don't respond.

"We should clean up," she says.

I shake my head no.

"Please, Malar."

I keep drawing. "I said no."

Priya shakes her head like she's giving up. I look up at Kamal, who's standing beside Priya.

Kamal still doesn't say anything. Then, in his eyes, I see tears.

That's when I know: he is sorry.

But sometimes you need to hear the words to move on. And I know that's not going to happen, so I continue drawing even when Priya and Kamal leave to shower and change into new clothes.

Everyone gathers in the backyard. Appa sits by a pottery wheel and adds finishing touches to a clay pot. Chithappa ties flowers, mango leaves, and a turmeric root around its neck.

Kamal is silent the entire time.

Amma enters the cowshed. "Oh, my dear Malar." She puts her arm around me. "I'm proud of you for not yelling at Kamal and Priya," she whispers into my ear.

I blink away my tears and hug her tight. "You knew what happened?"

Amma nods. "I know you, kanna," she says. "Now, let's celebrate with our family."

Her words release every big angry, sad, and guilty emotion I've been holding. I run inside and clean up. When I return, everything in the yard seems normal; it's almost as if nothing bad happened. Amma and Appa look happy. So do Chithi and Chithappa. So do Priya and Kamal.

So do Lakshmi and Gowri, in the cowshed. So do Raja and Rani, in the chicken coop.

"Let's gather around," Appa says.

Amma lights the flame on the mud stove under the sun. Appa places the pot on the stove. Into the pot goes rice, lentils, milk, jaggery, cardamom, cashews, raisins, and ghee. We wait and watch until the mixture boils, then overflows. Chithi lights the lamp. Chithappa circles the camphor around the sun.

Priya, Kamal, and I ring the bells.

"We honor Surya, the sun god, and reap the yields from our harvest," Amma says.

"Pongalo-Pongal!" everybody yells, and we bow to the sun.

My nostrils draw in the odors of rice, lentils, vegetables, and spices floating in the air. Amma never makes a simple lunch for festivals: there's pongal, vadai, kootu, and fifteen other items to eat.

We all sit on the ground together, forming a circle. Amma and Appa serve the food on banana leaves, and we have a grand feast. Sometime in the middle of lunch, Priya turns to me.

"I'm sorry we upset you. Truly."

Kamal joins her. "I'm sorry, Priya Akka, Malar Akka?"

The words come out of him in a rush. I look at Kamal and see regret in his face. I'm surprised by the word he used to address me. Akka. He called me his big sister. No one has ever called me Akka.

Priya says, "Friends? Please?"

"Akka?" he asks again. "Friends?"

When Kamal says "Akka," his face transforms into a blooming lotus like his name.

I lick the last bit of dessert off my fingers and let the sweetness linger on my tongue for longer than usual. "Friends," I say.

Chapter Eight

Maattu Pongal

WE ATE SO MUCH festival food yesterday that we all take our time waking up this morning. Priya, Kamal, and I are sprawled on the same straw mat together. I squint at the sun rays streaming through the window. I make shapes in the air with my fingers, and Priya peeks through them. The sound of our giggling fills the room.

"I'm sad that Pongal is over," Priya says.

"It's not!" I say. "We're only two days into the festival. There are still two more! Today is Maattu Pongal. It'll be so much fun."

"What are we going to do?" she asks.

"So many things!" I say.

Priya, Kamal, and I get out of bed and go to the backyard, where Amma and Chithi are waiting for us.

"Today we honor our cattle for all they do to feed and fulfill us," Amma says.

"Want to wash the cow and calf?" Chithi asks.

"Yeah," I say.

"Eww!" Priya squirms. "No way."

"I do. I do," says Kamal.

"Come on, Priya," I say as I tug her toward the cowshed.

But Priya pulls away. "They scare me."

"I'll go." Kamal follows me inside the shed.

"There's no need to be afraid. See?" I pat Gowri's rump. "Trust me. It will be okay."

Priya says it's stinky but joins us.

Lakshmi and Gowri swing their tails up and down. Amma attaches a hose to the tap and turns it on. I wet the cow and the calf starting at their heads. Amma and Chithi rub soap on their necks and backs.

I hand a small pail to Kamal. "Here. Do you want to help?"

He scrubs the animals' bellies and legs.

"I wanna try." Priya joins me and rinses all the soap from the top of Lakshmi before moving downward.

"Now comes the difficult part," Amma says. "Hold them, will you?"

I grab Lakshmi's halter. Chithi holds Gowri. Amma uses a gentle spray on the cows' faces. A splash of water here. A splash of water there.

SPLISH! SPLASH!

Water on our faces. Water on our clothes. Water everywhere.

"What a mess," Priya shouts.

Kamal roars with laughter.

Finally, finally, Priya pats Lakshmi. Then she pats Gowri, too.

While the animals dry in the sun, Appa gives us liquid colors—red, blue, green, yellow, and purple.

Appa and Chithappa hold Lakshmi and Gowri.

Chithappa calls out to us. "Come on, kids. This will be fun."

"And now we paint," I tell Priya and Kamal.

We take out brushes and stroke and splash their horns and hooves with colors. Then we dress the animals with bells, garlands, and vermilion powder.

The cow and the calf go *MMMBAAAAA!* and *JHILL-JHILL-JHUM-JHUM!*

Priya wipes the sweat off her brow. "This is a lot of work, but it's really fun, too."

"We're not done until we feed them," Appa says.

He gives us bananas and a pile of hay to feed to the animals.

While Kamal takes his turn feeding the cows, I put my arm around Priya's shoulders. "Know what I like about you?"

"What?" Priya asks.

"You're not as bossy as I thought you'd be. You can be annoying. But you can also be gentle and sweet, like a friend."

Priya leans toward me. "Sometimes, Malar, I thought you and I would never get along. And then you did so many things for me and Kamal. You're a good host," she says in my ear.

Amma brings out sugarcane sticks and pots full of pongal. We all take turns feeding Lakshmi and Gowri. Priya and Kamal drop a generous share of nuts in Raja and Rani's coop. The rooster and the hen are warming up to them. In the afternoon, we'll let Lakshmi, Gowri, Raja, and Rani roam free in the fields.

"There is a thiruvizha by the river today," Appa says.

I look over at Priya and Kamal. "That means lots of things to see, buy, eat, and do."

"Who wants to go?" Amma asks.

"Me," Priya says.

"Me too," Kamal echoes.

I raise my hand. "Me too!"

"Great!" Amma says. "But first, lunch."

Chapter Nine

Visiting the Local Fair

AFTER LUNCH, we walk along the riverbed. "Kaveri is the center of life in Pori," Appa says. "The river is where all the celebrations begin and end—where the most wonderful memories are made."

The midday sun promises a beautiful afternoon. In a normal year, we'd see hundreds of people arrive from the neighboring towns and villages. But this year, because of the cyclone, a much smaller crowd is celebrating near the shore.

Along the water, vendors sell clothing, jewelry, snacks, tender coconuts, and ice pops from carts. We see groups of people along the line of coconut trees bordering the river. The symphony of songs from loudspeakers vibrates in our ears.

We follow our parents toward the heart of the fair, where most of the crowd is gathered. The fragrances of incense and garlands of marigold, jasmine, and roses fill the air. Even though we've already had lunch, the aromas from fried snack foods—chili bajji and pakoda and vadai—and meals—idli, dosai, and tomato rice from the tarpaulin tents—make my mouth water.

Priya and Kamal can't resist touching the toys and clothes sold in all shapes, colors, and sizes.

Kamal spots some kites flying in the distance. "I want a kite. I want a kite," he says, and runs toward them.

"Wait, Kamal," Chithi shouts.

But he doesn't listen.

"Kamal! Kamal!" Priya cries.

We all run after Kamal, but we can barely keep up with him. Kamal goes to the very end of the stretch of vendor shops and stops by the man selling kites. Appa and Chithappa hustle forward until they reach him.

"All right, chellam," Appa says, grabbing his hand. "We must stick together."

Running under the hot sun made us sweaty. But thanks to Kamal's excitement, we each get kites.

Then we see many families gathered in a circle.

"What's going on here?" Priya asks.

"That's a game. Uriyadi," Appa says. "Usually we'd have several other games—silambam, the martial art; jallikattu, the bull race; and some others. But we just have the one this year."

When Priya sees the decorated clay pots suspended from a rope, and people holding sticks and canes, she yells, "Everyone's going to try to break the pots, right?"

"You know this game?" I ask, surprised.

"The pots are filled with candies, like piñatas, aren't they?"

"Candies. Candies. I want candies!" Kamal jumps and shouts.

"Almost. These pots have turmeric water in them. But you've taught me a new word. Pinni-atta."

Priya laughs and pronounces it again. "Pin-yah-tah," she corrects me. "And you call it . . . ooh what?"

"Oo-ree-yuh-dee," I say.

"Oo-ree-yuh-dee. Oo-ree-yuh-dee," Priya repeats.

"Want to play?" I ask her.

"I'm in. Let's go for it."

Kamal is too young, so just Priya and I stand in line with the other kids. Although I've played this game before, this time seems different. Maybe it's the presence of Priya—my new friend—that makes me excited to share it with her.

First, the organizer gives us long wooden canes. Then we're blindfolded and the organizer blows the whistle.

"Priya! Priya! Malar! Malar!" our family yells.

"Akka! Akka!" I hear Kamal's cheering voice.

"Go! Go! Go!"

"Wait!"

"Move left!"

"Move right!"

"Hit!"

The crowd is shouting out instructions, but there's so much noise that I can hardly hear anyone clearly. I stand on my tiptoes and move slowly.

I swing my cane in the air. Once. Twice. Three times. I don't break a pot in my three swings.

"I lost," I shout, and remove my blindfold. I'm out of the game, but I realize Priya is the only one still playing.

"Go, Priya!" I shout to her, and join my family.

Priya swings her cane once.

No good.

She swings her cane again and doesn't hit a pot.

"This is your final swing," the organizer announces.

Our voices grow louder. Chithappa and Appa hold out their phones, snapping pictures.

Kamal stands with his hands folded and begins to chant, "Akka! Akka!"

Priya moves a step closer to one of the hanging pots. My stomach forms a knot. She swings her cane hard.

She breaks the pot.

The turmeric water gushes out, soaking her. My arms break out in goose bumps.

"We have a winner!" the organizer announces, and gives Priya a garland of flowers.

We cheer and I hug her tight. Everybody claps.

"I can't believe I actually won something in Pori." Priya beams.

The joy on her face is worth a million stars.

Thank goodness Amma brought along extra clothes for us. After Priya changes, Chithappa gathers everybody together. "Just one more thing to do before we leave."

"Parisal?" I ask him.

"Right, podisu!" He gives me a high five.

"Haiya!" I clap. "You'll love boating in the river," I say to Priya and Kamal.

All of us get into the parisal, a round wicker boat, and the operator takes us for a ride. As we spin around, we laugh so much our stomachs hurt.

When we get back to the shore, we catch a glimpse of a huge chariot parading down the main street of the village.

"Look!" Kamal's eyes widen. "An elephant!"

"What's that on its trunk?" Priya asks.

"It's a gold caparison," I tell her. "And see the umbrella on its back?"

"It's beautiful," Priya shouts.

People sing, dance, and play all kinds of musical instruments. Chithi whistles and Amma claps while Appa and Chithappa dance. The colored lights from the chariot brighten our faces.

Amma gives us bananas to feed the elephant. One by one, we walk up to the elephant and place a banana in its trunk. The animal gobbles the fruit in an instant. Then it bows its head from side to side as if to say thank you.

"We have one more day. Just one more," I say to Priya as we walk back home at night.

"You sound desperate for more of your cousin Priya," she teases me. "Honestly, I can't believe we leave Pori tomorrow. I wish we could stay a few more days. But then we'll be off to explore other places in India, and you'll have your room to yourself again."

"All to myself," I say, and laugh.

She takes my hand in hers. "We had so much fun. I'm sorry if I hurt your feelings at first. I didn't mean to. I love that now we're friends."

Priya's words take me by surprise. Being a super-host to my cousins was hard. But now I'm beginning to feel I might have gotten the hang of it. "I love how you make your own choices instead of checking with your parents all the time. And you taught me to dance and to share." I brush my hair from my face. "And you broke the pot in Uriyadi. You are the GOAT!"

"No." Priya shakes her head. "You're the GOAT!"

Time is still for a moment, then we hug.

"Let's make the most of tomorrow," I say.

Kamal nudges me with his elbow. "What are we gonna do tomorrow?"

I ruffle his hair. "You'll just have to wait until morning."

When we get back home, Amma puts a movie on TV and we all sit around to watch it. Somewhere around the part where the hero and villain meet for the second time and fight, I look around the room. Kamal is lying on Amma's lap and enjoying tickles. Chithi and Appa are watching the movie. Chithappa is asleep in the easy chair.

Priya nudges me.

"I have a secret," she tells me.

"Oh! I'm bad at keeping secrets."

"But I have to share it with you, Malar. Or my head will burst," Priya pleads. "Come with me to the bedroom."

"Now?"

"Now." Priya drags me to my room and closes the door. She opens her suitcase and takes out a wrapped gift from underneath her clothes. "This is the secret that Kamal and I have been hiding from you all along. I wanted to give it to you on the last night we'd have together."

I open the gift. It's a pair of jeans.

I beam at Priya.

Priya seems determined to make me smile even more. She looks at my paintings hanging on the walls. "By the way, you're a good artist, too."

I show her all my paintings, even the incomplete ones—a tulsi plant, a swing, a banyan tree, children playing by the river.

"You've got to teach me how to draw a temple like that," she says.

I try to thank her, but words crumble and melt in my mouth like powdered sugar.

Chapter Ten

Kaanum Pongal

WE WAKE UP before sunrise the next day. The last morning of our celebration is here already: Kaanum Pongal, the day when we strengthen our relationships. It is also Thiruvalluvar Day, when we honor the celebrated Tamil poet Thiruvalluvar. I recite several couplets of his poetry, and Amma explains the meaning to Priya and Kamal as we help out in the kitchen. We make red rice and yellow rice and cut pieces of fruit and sugarcane.

Then we bring out the leftovers from yesterday's meal along with what we prepared this morning. We arrange turmeric leaves in a row under the sun and fill them with pongal, yellow rice, red rice, sugarcane, and stew.

Chithi sings and calls to the birds, "Kaakkai pidi vaikkiraen, kanu pidi vaikkiraen, kaakkaikum kuruvikkum kalyanam."

"The song means 'I keep food for the crows and sparrows. Today marks their wedding,'" I explain to Priya and Kamal.

"May we always live in harmony and stay united like the birds that flock together," Amma tells us.

"Kaaka! Kaaka! Kuruvi! Kuruvi!" All of us shout until groups of crows and sparrows fly down for bites.

And that is the end of the Pongal festival.

Amma looks down at us and grins. She extends her arms, and we do a group hug. "All good things must come to an end, darlings," she says. "And great things are waiting for us in the future. We'll have more special times as a family—I promise."

But I'm still sad that Pongal is over. I've begun to like the company of my cousins.

"Malar, we'll see each other again, okay?" Priya says in a soothing voice. "We'll come back here. You made us feel special, and we had so much fun."

I don't want her to be sad, too, so I give her a wide smile. "Let's play with our kites."

Chithappa, Chithi, and Appa hold up our kites until a mild wind blows. Then they let go. Up, up, up go our kites into the sky.

Kamal jumps up and down.

"Balance, chellam!" Appa cries.

"Pull, podisu!" shouts Chithappa.

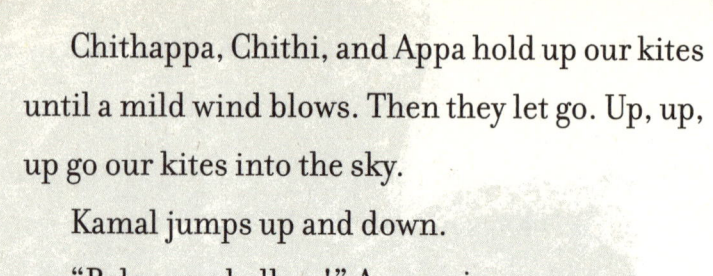

We pull on the lines hand over hand and run, holding the kites over our heads. They slowly catch the wind and soar into the sky. The higher the kites fly, the stronger they pull. We hold them for as long as we can, but the kites seem to have a will of their own. When the spools have unraveled

all of the string, Chithappa and Appa reel the kites in so they don't disappear into the bright sky.

Afterward, we head inside, and Chithi and Chithappa pack all their bags.

Before we realize, it's evening already. We step out into the backyard so Kamal and Priya can say their goodbyes to Lakshmi, Gowri, Raja, and Rani.

"Bye, Raja. See ya, Rani." Kamal waves.

When we go into the cowshed, Priya and Kamal walk toward the cow and calf, offering them banana leaves.

"Lakshmi, see what we brought for you," I say.

The animals munch on the leaves. "I never imagined we'd get so attached to them," Priya says, stroking Lakshmi's face while Kamal rubs Gowri's hide.

Chithi steps into the backyard. "Time to go, kids."

Priya sighs. She and Kamal give one last pat to the cow and calf. As we walk into the house, I notice their eyes well up, but they try hard not to cry.

In my bedroom, I slip a pair of glass bangles into Priya's hands. "Here's a gift for you."

"They're beautiful. Thank you for everything," Priya says. "You're the greatest host of all time! Give me a hug, girl."

I wrap my arms around her, and we hug.

I give Kamal a lollipop. "I'll miss you, my little sundaikka."

"Pop! Pop!" he cheers. I hide my sadness under a smile.

As we walk to the bus stop, I turn my back to Kamal and bend to his height. "Hop on, uppu mootai."

He jumps onto my back. I carry him while Priya walks beside us. She doesn't speak, and her eyes are glazed with tears.

At the bus stop, we say nothing. Priya and Kamal stand on either side of me with their arms around my shoulders. Then Kamal farts, and the three of us laugh so loud that everybody on the street stares. When the bus arrives, tears roll down our cheeks like ripples of the Kaveri River. We hold each other's hands and don't let go.

Chithi looks at me over her glasses. "Stay well, sweetie, and take care of the animals."

"Whistle podu, Chithi!" I wrap my arms around her waist. While she whistles, I cling to her tightly.

Chithappa gives me a fist bump. "Podisu, see you in Seattle soon!"

He loads up the bags. Amma, Appa, and I watch them board the bus. I keep waving until the bus slips away and is out of sight.

Somehow, I have never felt lonelier. A slice of our family left with Priya and Kamal.

"When can I see them again?" I ask Amma.

"Hopefully you won't have to wait that long, kanna," Amma says, giving me a hug.

"But until then, you can catch up with them over the phone and video chat," Appa says. "We're proud of you, Malar. You were a super-host. You treated your cousins well," he adds.

Missing Priya and Kamal is not like missing school or ice cream. It's harder. I miss their presence, their jokes, their accent, their faces. I miss the fun. I miss their company, their friendship, the way they held my hands before they boarded the bus.

When I get home, I put on the jeans that Priya gave me and pop the last truffle into my mouth. Then I open my box of colored paints. I take out a sheet of paper and start painting.

Filling the blank sheet in front of me is like filling the hole in my heart. I splash red, pink, blue, green, and yellow on the paper with my brush. It brings back the joy and gratitude of Pongal in a rainbow of colors.

When I'm finished, I show Appa and Amma.

"I'm going to send this to Priya and Kamal," I say to them. "Maybe Priya will say it's the GOAT!"

"I'm sure your cousins are missing you, too," Amma says.

I close my eyes. In the quiet of the room, I feel like I'm with Priya and Kamal, playing and holding their hands.

Missing is loving, too.

I can't wait to see Priya and Kamal again.

They are my family. And I'm theirs.

Glossary

aamaa (ah-MAH): yes
akka (UK-kah): older sister
amma (UM-mah): mother
appa (UP-pah): father
Atithi devo bhava (AH-tee-tee DAY-voh BAH-vah): Guests are equal to gods
badam (BAH-dahm): almond
badam paal (BAH-dahm pahl): spiced almond milk
bajji (BUH-jee): fried fritters in chickpea batter
Bargur (bar-GOOR): a breed of cattle native to western Tamil Nadu

Bhogi (BOH-gee): the first day of Pongal
chellam (chel-LUM): dear one
chithappa (chit-TUP-pah): uncle
chithi (CHIT-tee): aunt
chudidhar (CHUH-dee-dar): a two-piece garment that consists of a long tunic and a pair of fitted pants
Deepavali (dee-PAH-vuh-lee): the festival of lights, celebrated in the fall
dosai (DOH-sah-ee): crepe
dupatta (doo-PAHT-tah): a long scarf worn by women as part of the chudidhar outfit
ghee: Indian clarified butter
haiya (HAH-ee-yah): yay
haiyo (HAH-ee-yoh): gosh
idli (EED-lee): steamed rice and lentil cake
Indra (IN-drah): king of the gods
inga (EENG-guh): here
iruttu puyal (YEE-root-too puh-YEL): literally a dark storm; used to refer to a cyclone or similar large storm

jaggery: unrefined sugar

jallikattu (JUH-lee-KUT-too): bull or ox race in South India, involving both humans and animals

joot! (JUTE): go!

Kaanum Pongal (KAH-noom PONG-gul): the fourth and final day of Pongal

kandippa (KUN-dee-pah): surely

kanna (KUN-nah): dear

Kaveri (KAH-vay-ree): the name of a river in South India

kili-mooku seval (KIL-ee-MOH-kuh SAY-vul): parrot-beaked chicken

kolam (KOH-lum): a design or pattern that is drawn using rice flour, chalk, chalk powder, or rock powder in the thresholds of South Indian homes

kootu (KOO-tuh): lentil and vegetable stew

Maattuu Pongal (MAH-too PONG-gul): the third day of Pongal; honors cattle and farming livestock

Madurai malli (MUD-ray MUH-lee): jasmine flower from the city of Madurai

malar (muh-LER): flower

Mariamman (MAH-ree-um-mun): the mother goddess Mari

maruthaani (MUH-roo-DAH-nee): a tree leaf used to create temporary designs on the skin for festivals and special occasions

murukku (MOH-rook-koo): savory fried snacks made of rice and lentils

nadaswaram (NAH-dah-SWAH-rum): a type of wind instrument

naga (NAH-gah): snake

Nagaraja (nah-gah-RAH-jah): the king of snakes

neem: a type of tree that has antiseptic and medicinal benefits

paal (pahl): milk

pakoda (pah-KOH-dah): deep-fried vegetable fritters

parisal (pah-ree-SUL): a reed boat

paruthi paal (PAH-roo-th-ee pahl): cottonseed milk

podi! (POH-dee): go away, girl!

podisu (POH-dee-soo): little one

podu (POH-doo): whistling podu is a special kind of high-pitched whistling often used by soccer fans

pongal (PONG-gul): to boil; also the name of a rice dish as well as the harvest festival

Pongalo-Pongal! (PONG-gul-oh PONG-gul): an exclamation shouted at Pongal when the rice begins to boil and overflow its pot; it is a wish for everyone to share in plenty and good fortune in the year ahead

Pori (poh-REE): fictional village where Malar lives

Rajinikanth (RAJ-nee-KAHNTH): famous actor from South India

romba pazhasu (ROHM-buh PAH-zha-soo): very old; ancient

sambar (SAHM-bar): lentil soup

Sanskrit (suns-krit): ancient classical Indian language
silambam (see-LAHM-bum): a martial art in South India performed with a spear or a staff
Siva (see-VAH): the Hindu god of destruction
sundaikka (SOON-dah-kah): turkey berry
Surya (SOO-riyah): god of the sun
Thai Pongal (tah-ee PONG-gul): the second day of Pongal
thalaiva (TAH-lay-vah): head or leader of a group
thambi (TAHM-bee): younger brother
thavil (TAH-veel): a type of drum
Thiruvalluvar (TEE-roo-VAHL-loo-vahr): Indian poet and philosopher best known for his work *Tirukkural*, a collection of poetic couplets on various subjects
thiruvizha (TEE-roo-VEE-zhah): a fair in a village or small town
uppu mootai (OO-poo MOO-tah-ee): a sack filled with salt

uriyadi (OO-ree-yuh-dee): a game similar to piñata played in South India

Uzhavar Thirunal (OO-zhuh-var Tee-roo-naal): Farmers' Day; another name for Thai Pongal, the second day of Pongal

vaa (vah): come (to one person)

vaanga (VAHNG-kah): come (to several people or to an elder)

vadai (vah-DAH-ee): fried lentil dumplings

vanakkam (VAHN-nuk-kum): a greeting

Varuna (VAH-roon-uh): the god of rains

vendakkai (VEN-duh-KAH-ee): okra

veshti (VESH-tee): a wrapped garment worn on the lower body

yogi (YOH-gee): a person who practices yoga

zari (ZUH-ree): gold or silver thread usually embroidered on clothing

Author's Note

PONGAL IS A HOLIDAY in India celebrating the harvest. In South India, it takes place over four days in mid-January during the Tamil month called Thai, in honor of the hard work farmers do. The harvest festival symbolizes a season of hope and renewal.

The first day of Pongal is called Bhogi Pandigai. The second day is the most important day, and it's called Thai Pongal. It is also called Uzhavar Thirunal, which means Farmers' Day. The third day is called Maattu Pongal. The last day is called Kaanum Pongal. The festival brings families and friends together to celebrate the blessings of good health and happiness.

Pongal means "to boil" in Tamil. It is also the name of the rice dish that is prepared for this festival. We make two types of pongal on the second day of the festival—one sweet and the other savory. It is served with a stew made with the season's vegetables.

Pongal marks the end of the winter solstice and the beginning of the sun's six-month journey up to Earth's Northern Hemisphere. Solstices are a planet's longest and shortest days of the year. The longest day marks the beginning of summer and is called the summer solstice. The shortest day marks the beginning of winter and is called the winter solstice.

The harvest festival is also celebrated in many parts of India at other times of the year than the solstice. It goes by different names depending on the region—Sankranti, Lohri, Kanumu, Bihu, Poki, Hadaga, or Onam.